Camping

A Mr. and Mrs. Green Adventure

K E I T H   B A K E R

sandpiper

HOUGHTON MIFFLIN HARCOURT
Boston   New York

The text of this book is set in Giovanni Book.
The illustrations were done in acrylic paint on illustration board.

The Library of Congress has cataloged *Meet Mr. and Mrs. Green* as follows:
Baker, Keith, 1953–
Meet Mr. and Mrs. Green/Keith Baker
p. cm
"Book Four."
ISBN: 978-0-15-204954-6 hardcover
ISBN: 978-0-15-204955-3 paperback
Summary: A loving alligator couple enjoys themselves
as they go camping, eat pancakes, and visit the fair.
[1. Alligators—Fiction] I. Title.
PZ7.B17427Me 2002
[E]—dc21 2001001955

ISBN: 978-0-547-74961-7 paper over board
ISBN: 978-0-547-74559-6 paperback

Manufactured in Mexico
RDT 10 9 8 7 6 5 4 3 2

4500378098

For my parents,

the first Mr. and Mrs. Green

It was Saturday morning.
It was sunny,
and it was hot.
"Let's go camping,"
said Mrs. Green.

Mr. Green had never
been camping.
He was excited.
Life with Mrs. Green
was full of adventure.

"We need a tent," said Mrs. Green.

"A big tent!" said Mr. Green.

"With lots of room."

"We need sleeping bags,"
said Mrs. Green.

"We need food and water,"
said Mrs. Green.

"We need warm clothes,"
said Mrs. Green.

"And pillows!"
said Mr. Green.
"Soft and fluffy pillows."

"Like chocolate bars
and marshmallows,"
said Mr. Green.
"And soda pop!"

"And bunny slippers!"
said Mr. Green.

Mrs. Green continued checking her list.

"We need a camp stove.

We need boots.

We need a first-aid kit.

We need flashlights.

We need matches.

We need hats.

We need a harmonica." (Mr. Green was a musician.)

"We need paints and paper." (Mrs. Green was an artist.)

"And . . . we need a map."

"A map?" asked Mr. Green.
"We need a map?"

"Yes, this map," said Mrs. Green.
"I made it last night."

Mr. Green began to worry.
We're going far away,
he thought.
There could be
dark, mysterious woods,
strange, eerie sounds,

spooky, glowing eyes,
sharp, pointy teeth,
and mosquitoes!
Mr. Green was not excited anymore.
He was scared.
And he hated mosquitoes.

But Mrs. Green wasn't scared.
She was ready to go.

Mr. and Mrs. Green hiked over their
welcome mat and down their front steps,

past Mr. Marble's rock garden
and his barking dog, Boulder,

beside their favorite picnic spot
(where Mr. Green once ate six watermelons),

across Polliwog Bridge
(the best fishing spot in town),

around every pothole and
dandelion in Shortcut Alley,

and through a squeaky back gate that
looked (and sounded) very familiar.

Mrs. Green pulled out her map.

"We will camp here," she said,
"next to the birdbath."

Mr. Green looked closely at the map.

He saw the path they had just traveled.

It ended at their backyard—

their cozy, comfortable, beautiful backyard.

Mr. Green was excited again.
The grass around the birdbath
was thick and soft.

It was the perfect place
to set up their tent.
He would sleep like a salamander.

After dinner they crawled into their sleeping bags.

"Look at that moon!" said Mrs. Green.

"It's like a giant marshmallow," said Mr. Green.

He began to play his harmonica.

But he fell asleep before finishing even one song.

Mrs. Green felt happy.
The sleeping bag was snuggly,
the stars were twinkling,
the frogs were croaking.
And best of all, Mr. Green
was snoring loudly by her side.